IN THE SHADOW OF LIGHT

ELAINE L. ORR

Copyright © 2018 Elaine L. Orr

All rights reserved.

ISBN-13: 978-1-948070-12-6

DEDICATION

To those who care and

teach their children to do the same.

ACKNOWLEDGMENTS

Thanks to friends Angela H. Myers and Diane Orr-Fisher who quickly read drafts of *In the Shadow of Light*, and to J.D. Webb, for naming Corozón.

Elaine L. Orr

CHAPTER ONE
COROZÓN

Friday, somewhere in Northern Mexico

"Corozón, you have to keep up."

"I'm trying Mamá." I want to say the dust burns my eyes and makes it hard to see. The aching tiredness makes it hard to walk. The dryness in my mouth means I can't easily gulp the air to walk fast. But I have to.

It's harder for Mamá. She has Pico tied to her back. He used to ride in the backpack, but when she washed our clothes in a creek, someone took it. We lost two bananas and his wooden donkey. He cried for hours for the toy.

When the bad men killed Papi, we knew we had to leave our village. Mamá helped him in our food store, Tienda de Sanchez, but she couldn't run it alone. And the bad men would want protection money from her, too. Mamá said the store will not exist for long. Every time the bad men killed people, the store made less money.

Mamá says in America we will be safe. Tito, father of my Papi, helped the American soldiers training Honduran soldiers, especially Colonel Bill. He would have died if Tito had not helped him in the jungle.

This was before I was born, but Colonel Bill said if we needed to come to America, he would help.

I try to walk faster, but my sandal hits the edge of a rock. I fall. I put out my hand, but the side of my face hits the stinging sand.

Mamá runs back to me. "Corozón, baby, you have to get up! The coyote won't wait."

I used to think coyotes were only the animals that tried to eat our baby goats. Now I know they are men who will lead us to America. They want to eat all of our money. I don't like the way our coyote looks at me.

Mamá helps me stand and brushes the front of my dusty dress. She sees I am trying not to cry, and kisses my stinging cheek. "Come, Baby. Hold my hand." We walk faster. I am almost running.

I, Corozón Sanchez, am ten years old. I have long, black hair, and am very pretty. Mamá says this is why I have to always walk just behind her. She says bad men may want to hurt me. I stay close to Mamá.

We walk at night and sleep under the scrub bushes during the day. Sometimes when I sleep I see the bad man put the knife in Papi. Mamá says when I see that to think of the pretty flowers we planted on his grave, not why he had to be buried.

It is almost daybreak. I know it will be hot, but I am so tired I will sleep. Before the sun is up, I see the sky in America looks sort of pink. Mamá says it is the lights from the big city of El Paso. She says America is so bright, even when it is dark.

After one more sleep, we have one more night to walk, and we will be in America. We will be safe. We will be free.

CHAPTER TWO
KYRA

Friday, Maryland, near DC

My tenth birthday party was supposed to be the most special. I reminded Mommy, and she says it will be fine with cake and ice cream. She is too busy with the new baby to shop for special decorations. I tell her I understand.

But I don't. I help with BabyJack all the time. When Mommy is so tired she says she could drop, I read my books next to his crib. If he wakes up I pat him on the back. If he still cries, I get Mommy.

I cried tonight, but into my pillow. I didn't know Daddy would hear me. He works so late, he's never home when it's light outside.

My Daddy is very important. He works for the president. He used to say he helped people, but when he said that when he was leaving for work last week, Mommy started crying really hard. Daddy stayed until she stopped.

He doesn't talk about his work now. It's still important, but when he talks about it, Mommy thinks about how he's never home. That's what I think, anyway.

But tonight Daddy hears me crying, and he says he will make it better. I tell him about the streamers at the party store, and the hats and napkins that are the same color. He'll buy them Saturday morning, before the party.

Because I'm such a good big sister.

CHAPTER THREE
THE JEFE

Friday, Washington, DC

"Damn it, I need those porta potties to be there before all the tents are up!"

I slam down the phone and close my eyes for several seconds. My hard-working mother taught me that. Every day she rode the bus to her job selling shoes ("touching other people's feet all day"), and when the bus was hot or someone shoved her, she shut her eyes and took a breath.

Sarah taps lightly on my door. "Mr. Danbury? Everything okay in there?"

I sit up straighter and pick up my pen to pretend to write something in the notebook I always have on my desk. "Come in Sarah."

When she enters my office, I smile. Sarah is the best part of my day. No one could have a better executive assistant. "I shouldn't yell at these contractors. It's not how my mother raised me."

She shrugs. "They're on mañana time, I suppose. I'm heading down to buy a sandwich. May I bring you something?"

I say no. Sarah won't think I'm being sexist by asking her to bring me lunch, but my deputy probably would. You can't trust civil servants.

My smart phone buzzes and a message from the public affairs chief pops up. McKenzie's always afraid he'll say the wrong thing and get canned. "WPR poking around. Has heard about new camps. Advise?"

This time I swear out loud. I know which *Washington Post* reporter he's talking about. Sam Wolfe has been dogging my ass since we started separating parents and children as the bastards sneak into our country. Let them take his job, see how he feels.

I reply, "Tell him u heard same rumor, and it's only that."

And I wish that were true. The adults we can cram anywhere, but I need more space for the kids and it can't be near populated areas. Don't want the effing liberals to get close too easily.

I turn to grab a Diet Coke from the small refrigerator on my credenza, and see the photo of my curly-haired daughter holding her tiny brother. "Yikes. Gotta get those streamers tomorrow morning." I add that to the list on the back page of my notebook.

CHAPTER FOUR
THE REPORTER

Friday, Washington, DC

I try not to let my impatience show. "Listen, McKenzie, this source is impeccable. He, or she, says you're going to build a new camp somewhere off Interstate 10 in west Texas, and it'll house 1,000 kids between ages three and ten."

I curse to myself. I shouldn't have given him that much detail. It could identify the deputy director of immigrant removal.

After a two or three second pause, McKenzie says, "I've been hearing that rumor all morning. I think it was started by a reporter at the *San Francisco Chronicle*."

"Huh?"

"You know what California's like. They hate the president. Rumors like that sell papers."

I'm pretty sure that his two-second pause means I'm on the right track, so I thank him politely and hang up. I buzz my editor on the internal phone line. "McKenzie says no, but not fast enough. My source says south of I-10, not too long a drive from El Paso. I'm gonna stay on it."

"Sure, just don't forget the piece on border wall funding."

I wish I could. I hang up and dial the intern who's doing some research for me. "Can you keep hounding your intern friend on the House Homeland Security Committee? We need better info on how the border wall negotiations are going."

"Sure thing. Bunch of us are meeting at The Dubliner at six. None of the committee staff will hear him talking to me."

I keep myself from saying I hope they aren't listening to him now. "Great. Keep me posted." The eager twenty-year old will do just that. He'd swab floors in the men's room to get a job at the *Post*.

Two PM. Enough time to snag a plane reservation to El Paso and hit the trail Saturday morning.

CHAPTER FIVE
THE COLONEL

Friday, Houston, Texas

I didn't used to drink beer until five. Since this president started rounding up kids, I moved it up to noon.

I lay my head on the patio table. Why can't I get the picture out of my mind? That crying little girl in the red shirt, standing in front of a man wearing blue latex gloves. Like she's the one who's dirty.

Honduran kids like that cried when the Morazanista Patriotic Front attacked their parents. But this is America. How can it happen here?

"Bill?"

I lift my head and focus on my wife. Annie doesn't deserve a drunk for a husband. "Hey, babe."

She smiles, but I see the worry in her eyes.

"Can I make you something to eat?"

Translation: "You're drinking already? We better get something in your stomach."

"That'd be great. How about one of your famous grilled bologna and cheese sandwiches?"

She wrinkles her nose at me and the worried eyes smile for a second. In junior high home ec class, she and another girl created what they called "bolocheese sandwiches." She won't feed them to our dog now, but I can't resist reminding her.

"Grilled cheese and chips coming up."

I don't put my head on the table again. I stare at our neatly trimmed back yard, with Annie's purple and yellow irises planted along the edge of our wood fence.

This is America. It's the man in the latex gloves who doesn't deserve our freedoms. I suppose it's his bosses who put him there. I wonder if he likes grabbing those kids.

Some days I wish I'd never come home from that humid jungle.

CHAPTER SIX
COROZÓN

Friday night, Northern Mexico

Mamá wakes me up after darkness has come. I sit up and ask her why we slept so late.

She tells me she and Pico didn't, but she let me sleep because we will start our walk later today. She checks my cheek. It still stings from my fall yesterday. She puts water on the hem of her skirt and pats my cheek with it.

"Are we close?"

She nods. "That's why we start late today. We have to do all our walking when it is dark."

Pico toddles to me, rests his hands on my knees, and drools. I pull him onto my lap and play peek-a-boo.

Our coyote calls out. "Walk fast, and if lights come from helicopters or searchers, lie flat on the ground."

He has not told us this before. I don't like it. Mamá says we don't need to worry. The coyote says this way works fastest, and the police in Estados Unidos are good, not like at home.

"Mamá. How do we find Colonel Bill?"

"He lives in Houston. Part of Texas." She nods her head. "We will find him. When they give us the asylum, we will find him."

Our coyote is nearby. He hears Mamá and gives me his thin smile. "Si. The asylum."

I am only ten, but I know this man is not our friend. When we had traveled for two days, he told Mamá the money from selling Tienda Sanchez was not enough for our journey. Mamá tells him again she had to sell very fast, and take much less money than the store was worth.

The coyote does not care. He says she should give him her wedding band. Mamá did. She says she had no choice. We have no home to go back to.

I stand and help Mamá arrange Pico on her back. He wants to walk, and she finally has to slap his foot to get him to be still. It makes her tears come, but she wipes them away. Pico stops crying and drools on her shoulder.

We walk fast tonight. When I can see Mamá's face, her lips move. She is praying. I ask her if she prays to Papi. She says to God, and she thinks Papi is in heaven praying for us.

I am so thirsty, but we do not stop. The lights from El Paso are brighter. The coyote tells us we will go to the east of the city. We have seven more kilometers, he says. And we are not to talk.

After almost an hour we slow down and then stop. We are twenty people, and the coyote talks to each family. We have been walking single-file, and he tells us to spread out, perhaps twenty paces between us. Mamá insists I walk with her, and he does not like this. She holds my hand tighter.

After perhaps fifteen minutes of walking spread out, he tells us we are in America. We are 10 kilometers east of El Paso. He turns and runs, very fast, back into Mexico.

Mamá is angry, but I am happy he is gone. Some of the men begin to run faster into America.

Mamá still holds my hand, and we look at each other. She tries to smile. "We will find the asylum ourselves." Soon, the others are gone. We go alone.

We walk for a few minutes when we see the lights. Cars I think. Mamá says no, maybe jeeps. Ahead, I hear shouts, but I don't know the words. I speak a little English, but not these words.

The lights get closer, and Mamá waves one hand above her head. She says these people will help us.

When the three men get out of their jeep, I know they are not our friends. The one in the middle begins to point a gun at us. Then he hears me cry for Mamá and sees her face. It is her fear face. Pico starts to cry. The man puts the gun in a leather pocket on his hip.

In English, Mamá says, "We are here for the asylum. They kill my husband because he and his father help the American Air Force man. Please help us."

Her request makes the men look at each other and talk very fast English. I don't think even Mamá understands.

Finally, the man in the middle smiles. In Spanish, he says, "You must be very tired. Why don't you put the baby down, and we will give you some water."

Mamá's smile is big. The man starts to help her with Pico, but Mamá says I know how to do it. While I unfasten Pico and put him on the ground next to me, the man who reminds me of the coyote gets a bottle of water from their jeep.

Mamá thanks him for the water. First she stoops to hold the bottle for Pico to have a sip, then me. Then she stands up and takes a long drink for herself. She smiles again at the men. "*Mucha gracias.*"

The next things happen very fast. The man with the water takes Mamá's arm and tells her to stand still.

Her voice rises. "*Qué pasa?*"

The man who had his gun out before turns toward Pico. I move faster than I ever have. I pull Pico to me, with one of his legs on each side of my waist. I hold onto him very tight, and tell him to hold onto me.

Pico screams, but he holds onto me.

Mamá calls out that Colonel Bill from Houston is a friend to us.

Some lights flash on my right, and the man who showed us his gun starts to run toward the flashes. Another man tells him to stay.

In Spanish, the man who has not talked before now says, "Let go, chica, we will help you."

I do not let go. I will never let anyone take my Pico from me.

CHAPTER SEVEN
KYRA

Saturday, Maryland, near DC

It is my best birthday ever. Daddy did not go to work this Saturday. He says he will stay home until two o'clock. My party is from eleven until one o'clock. He will be here the entire time.

Mommy is still very tired, but she smiles a lot. My friends' parents have brought sandwiches and pretzels, a surprise. They tell Mommy to let them serve the cake and ice cream.

Daddy makes everyone laugh. We play Pin the Tail on the Donkey. It's a silly game, but fun. Daddy says we can use him for the donkey. Mommy giggles and says to use the donkey on the cork board she set up.

When BabyJack needs a nap, it's time for the party to be over. That's why the party was from eleven to one o'clock.

Bethany wants me to come to her house to play. Mommy and Daddy say okay, but not to stay long. "You've had a full day, pumpkin."

When Daddy isn't looking, I roll my eyes at Bethany. Her Daddy calls her Carrot Top, because of her red hair. We think the vegetable names are funny.

Bethany's brother is six months older than BabyJack. Her mother will walk home before us, so she can put him down for his nap. Then Bethany and I will walk the four houses to Bethany's.

We will play quietly during nap time. We are both always good.

Bethany won the prize for Pin the Tail on the Donkey. The stuffed bear is as big as her brother, but not as heavy. She carries that and I carry her party favors. We stop in front of her house because she wants to get the tiara from her bag of favors, to wear for her Daddy.

The blue van looks like the one our teacher has. We wave as the side door slides open. But it isn't Mrs. Peabody.

The man's face looks squished, and the man who comes out behind him looks the same. Then I remember one of the news reports Daddy watched. A man who robbed a bank had stockings on his face. Like the ones Mommy wears, but over his face.

Bethany knows they are bad, too. She drops her bear and turns toward her house. But the first man grabs her and lifts her. He runs to the van.

I want to scream but I can't. The second man picks me up. He puts his hand over my mouth, and jumps into the van with me.

The van door shuts and the man who has me yells, "Hurry the hell up!"

The van is dark inside. Something is on the windows to make it dark. The van drives away very fast. I think I hear someone outside the van shouting, but I'm not sure.

Then the men put us on the floor and lie on top of us. They both say the same thing. "Be quiet and you won't get hurt!"

CHAPTER EIGHT
THE JEFE

Saturday, Maryland, near DC

The police came first, then the FBI. Then the doctor, to give my Angela a shot. He says she can't breastfeed for two days, but I tell him we have formula. Anything so Angela can stop crying and throwing up.

I want to cry and throw up, too, but someone has to deal with this. Has to remember what part of our lives can be connected to the kidnappers, can help the FBI find our daughter.

For a time, Bethany's parents, Hal and Jordan, sat in our living room with us and the FBI. Then the agents said we needed to be in our separate homes, because ransom demands can come to either place.

Two hours later, the FBI has no leads, but they do have a theory. My role in separating children from their parents at the U.S. border with Mexico. Though the first agent to broach it said 'seizing.'

Now I wanted to throw up. Sure, plenty of Twitter nuts wished the president and attorney general would end the practice. I didn't like working on it. I told myself it was for the greater good. But to kidnap my daughter?

And why take Bethany? Because she was with Kyra?

I let the agent's words sink in. "My job. I mean, I know a bunch of Democrats are angry, but…"

The female agent asks, "Democrats?"

The agent-in-charge says, "Agent Saldano. Focus."

Face red with what looks like fury, she says, "I'm very focused on finding these two children."

The agent standing just inside our front door adds, "The border separations may be unconnected, but you have to see the irony. You're a key player in pulling these children away from their parents. They preached against it at my church last week."

I wish I had received a shot.

In a loud voice, the agent-in-charge says, "Mr. Delaney."

I realize he said it a moment before and I didn't answer. "What? What should I do?"

"You need to go over every minute of the last few weeks. Did anyone you don't know stop you on the street? To talk about anything, but especially the seizures."

"I…no. I drive to the Department of Justice, and I have a parking space under the building."

More calmly, Agent Saldano asks, "So you tend mostly to see people you know?"

The door agent asks, "What about in the neighborhood? Do you stop at the grocery store on the way home, anything like that?"

"My wife…the grocery store delivers. I mean, not usually, but since the new baby…"

In the background, I become aware of the phone ringing. It has been ringing often. An agent takes the calls.

This time they bring me the phone. Angela's parents want to drive to Maryland from New Jersey. At the FBI's urging, I ask them to wait a day. Then an agent gets on the phone and says someone will be at their home in a few minutes to see if they have any ideas.

Tears well in spite of my best efforts. I've only been doing my job. We use air conditioned places for the children, even the tents. We ask them about food allergies.

I look at the agent in charge. "What do we do now?"

He stares at me for a moment and looks away. "We wait."

The agent at the door says, "Prayer never hurts."

CHAPTER NINE
THE REPORTER

Saturday, El Paso

When the plane lands in El Paso Saturday morning, I have nineteen new voice-mails. Eleven are from my editor. "Christ. He knew I was on the plane."

He minces no words. "Joseph Delaney's daughter and a friend have been kidnapped."

"What? DOJ Joe Delaney?"

"No, the one who works at Disneyland. CNN is sayin' it's because of his role in seizing the kids. I think it's a guess. What do you hear?"

"I just got off the plane. I'll work the phones and call you back."

I sit in a chair by the arrival gate and think for two full minutes. Then I pull up the CNN and CBS web pages to see what they have. Nothing but talking heads and speculation. Same with Fox News, though they are presenting the kidnapping as part of a plot to damage the president.

The idea of kidnapping a child to protest government policies? I look at the CNN site again. Two kids, one possibly in the wrong place at the wrong time.

My phone buzzes. A Texas area code. I answer as I begin to walk to the airport exit, en route to my rental car.

In Spanish-accented English, a man says, "You Sam Wolfe from the *Washington Post*?"

"The one and only as far as I know."

"I took some photographs last night. You need to see them."

It takes me an hour to get to the man on the northern edge of El Paso. He only told me his first name – Juan – in case my calls are monitored. He says he is a nobody, so no one will be tapping his calls.

The grungy bar matched my mood, and his photographs tear at my core. A little girl clinging to a much younger child, a boy, I think. A woman screaming as Border Patrol agents haul her away. Two agents trying to separate the children.

Juan studies my face. "I think my camera's flash made them stop pawing at the kids. They threw them on the floor of their SUV together. Carted the woman off in another one."

My body heat is from more than the stifling temperature. "Were you close enough to hear anything?"

"Just a few words. Something about Colonel Bill in Houston. And I think asylum."

"Colonel? Not uncle or something?"

"If he was their uncle, they would say *Tio Guillermo*. And if he were a colonel in a Mexican or Central American Army, they'd have probably said *el coronel*. They used an English pronunciation. And name, of course."

I look up from the photos. "So, maybe an American they know?"

Juan shrugs. "Maybe. It's a start."

"Mexican kids, you think?"

Juan shrugs again. "I'd say farther south. From what little I heard, the accent sounded like Honduran or Ecuadoran. But I'm maybe wrong."

"So Juan…"

He smiles. "It really is Juan. Gomez."

We shake hands again. "Okay, how can I work with you?" I deliberately did not say, "What do you want from me?"

"I want this story in the *Post*. I'd like to be paid for it. And I want the evil to stop."

"Of course. This is..." I glance again at the photo of the children gripping each other, "explosive."

Juan nods. "And I think you'd have the clout to look for a Colonel Bill."

I agree. "We've had a lot of troops in Central America."

"No kidding. I can help you, but I live here, and I freelance. No protection from a paper or news station. I'll feed you what I can."

"You really think...?"

"Of course I think. I'm a citizen, born here. But I have a DACA cousin. She'd be easy to go after."

CHAPTER TEN
THE COLONEL

Saturday, Houston, Texas

The photo on the *Washington Post* web page shakes me to my core. All over Central and South America, kids know to be afraid of most police. These two now know to be scared of uniforms and badges in the United States. Their expressions are terror personified.

"Bill, look at the woman."

I glanced at Annie, who stands over my shoulder, staring at the computer screen. "What about her?"

"Wait a minute." She walk to a shelf in our family room and takes out what we called our international album. Photos of people we met during my tours overseas, when Annie was allowed to join me. I took a few when I deployed alone, but mostly she was the photographer.

She plopped the now-open album in front of me and points. A wedding picture.

"Who?" I study the photo and read the caption. "Tito's son. In Honduras."

She nods. "The son of the man who saved your life."

I remember a lot from that day in 1990. My Air Force Unit was training Honduran soldiers and pilots to respond to internal terrorist attacks. But that day, that was a good day. Two of the Hondurans had taken us to dinner at their family home.

The Inspector General report postulated that the ambush had been planned with the men whose homes we visited. I doubted it, and since they were the sole casualties, we couldn't ask them.

What I don't remember is what happened after the piercing sting in my leg. A direct hit to my femoral artery. While my unit members chased the attackers, I lay bleeding out on the warm Honduran ground. I remember a kindly face peering at me, and then nothing.

I woke up not in the Soto Cano Air Base hospital but in some sort of Honduran medical clinic. As I opened my eyes, a woman's voice, in heavily accented English, said, "We help you, but you must not speak."

Later, Tito told me I nodded and then passed out again. The next time I woke up, I was in the base hospital. Tito and his son, the man in the wedding photo – but a boy then – had rushed to me to staunch the bleeding. At great risk to themselves and their family, they carried me to a clinic several kilometers away.

Through some sort of almost clandestine network, they sent word to the base, and I was removed that night. The hope was that no one would know Tito and Manuel Sanchez had been the ones to save me.

Annie tapped my shoulder. "Bill? Can this be her, Manuel's wife?"

I compare the two photos again. "Hard to tell, she's so happy in the one, and terrified…"

Annie gasps. She had scrolled down, and now points to the screen. "The photographer heard the woman ask for Colonel Bill."

I stare at the monitor. "In Houston."

Annie shuts the album. "We have to find her."

"And the kids."

Annie's voice breaks. "You know the bastards took the children from her. They could be anywhere."

CHAPTER ELEVEN
COROZÓN

Early Saturday Morning, El Paso Sector

Pico threw up on me two times when we were on the floor of the jeep. Or whatever it was. We bumped so much my head hurt. But I held tight to Pico.

Our jeep has two men. One sits on the seat in the back and sometimes puts his hand on my back. But they talk in English. I only know they are very angry at me for holding onto Pico.

Sometimes I can see street lights as we drive through towns. The rest of the time, darkness covers us. Even the moon seems to be in shadow.

After a long time, maybe more than an hour, the dark of the roadway turns into bright lights. Lights everywhere. And lots of voices.

The men open the doors and get out of the jeep. Pico sleeps under me. Every inch of my arms feel cramped from holding him so tightly. I loosen my grip to relax for a few moments, and I start to shiver very hard.

Men yell. And then a woman speaks, loudly, first in English. As the men respond, she switches to Spanish. *"Los niños? Donde?"*

They must have told her children were in the jeep. The woman's voice grows closer, asking questions in rapid Spanish. How old are we? Don't they know babies go to the other center?

Her head and shoulders come into the back seat. "My God. You couldn't stop to clean them up? They're covered in vomit."

In Spanish, one of the men says so is his shoe. If they speak Spanish, why had they only spoken English to me?

The woman leans in, probably to get me out.

I yell. "This is my baby Pico. You can't have him!"

She draws back, but just a little. Then she says, "You can keep him. I will take you to the bathroom, and get you some clean clothes."

I look up at her, and my gaze falls on her gun.

She looks into my eyes. "The gun is not for you."

"The bad men took my Mamá."

"What is your name?"

I don't want to tell her. But maybe if I do I can keep Pico. "Corozón."

The woman speaks to the men behind her. "It means heart in Spanish. She probably thinks you have none."

She turns back to me. "Pico can stay with you tonight. Come. You must be hungry. And you're cold."

What choice did I have? When I climb out of the jeep and see the rolls of wire surrounding the compound, I know I have none. All I can do is hope this woman will let me keep my Pico.

He still sleeps, so he is very hard to carry. But I will not give him to the woman. She walks beside me, her hand on my shoulder.

She opens a door for us, and a man says something to her in English. In Spanish, she says, "It will wake up the other kids. I'll clean her up in here."

As she shuts the door, I see that 'here' is a nice place. The floor has carpet, and the air is cool. I know about air conditioning, but I am almost never in it. I sneeze.

The woman sticks her head out the door. "Bring me clothes, and diapers. Girls medium. And the boy is maybe one year old."

"His birthday is in four days."

She smiles at me. My first smile in America.

She has only paper towels, so it takes her many minutes to clean us. We have the dust from walking, and Pico's vomit. I hated the smell.

A man's voice speaks English, and she reaches outside the door to get some clothes and a piece of foil. I can tell it is something warm and heavenly.

She sees my eyes, and now Pico's. Washing has made him wake up.

She opens the foil and takes out two warm, flour tortillas. We usually ate corn tortillas, but I don't care.

The woman tears off small pieces for Pico. He eats two bites, and lies on the floor. She yells to the men outside. "What did you give them to drink?"

When no one answers, she says, "Bring me a coke. He acts like a kid about to pass out." She reaches to the top of the sink and gets a plastic cup, which she fills with water and hands to me.

Pico looks from the water to me, and then to the woman. "Pico needs water, too," I say.

"Just a sip. We'll give him Coke in a minute. It's better for his tummy."

After Pico has some Coke, he smiles at me. My second smile in America. I kneel next to him and kiss his cheek.

He touches my hand. "Mamá?"

I shrug. "Pico has Corozón."

He chews on a tortilla, staring at me and then the woman.

I dare to ask the woman a question. "Where is Mamá?"

She hesitates. "Perhaps with your papa."

When I start to cry, she says. "I don't know, I don't know. Do you know where your Papa is?"

"The bad men killed him. Will the American banditos kill Mamá, too?"

CHAPTER TWELVE
KYRA

Saturday, somewhere near DC

Bethany cries more than I do. I lie on the floor next to her, and try to pat her forehead. She pulls away.

"You have to be quiet. They say we can stay in this pretty room if we're quiet."

"I want Mommy and Daddy." But she says it softly.

"I want mine, too. But they showed us those ropes. Do you want to be tied up?"

She hiccups, but slowly stops crying. Bethany shakes her head.

I look around the room again. A door leads to a bathroom, and the only window is very high, almost like a skylight. The single bed has a doll and several books. I stand up and walk to the bed. "They have a Harry Potter book. The first one."

She sits up and sniffs. "That's the only one my mom let me read so far."

One bed. They didn't think Bethany and I would be together. We were in front of her house. Had they planned to take only her?

But we started at my house. Did they want me? Or just any ten-year-old girl? I am suddenly very cold, and I cross my arms to stop shivering.

Bethany stands up. "There's only one bed."

I nod. "I guess we can share."

Someone knocks at our door. Bethany and I hug each other.

A man's voice says, "I'm coming in. I won't hurt you. Please stay back from the door."

The knob turns and a man enters. Instead of the stockings, he has a black face mask with holes for his eyes, but not one for his mouth. The men who took us were smaller. Or maybe he was the driver.

He carries a small tray with plastic jars of apple juice, sandwiches, and two chocolate chip cookies. But not homemade.

"Hello Kyra, hello Bethany."

We say nothing. He moves toward us and we back up.

"I won't hurt you. I'll put the tray on the bed." And he does.

I decide to be brave. "We want to go home."

He nods. "We'll take you back in a day or two. We'll even give you pretty new clothes to wear home."

Bethany's eyes fill with tears and one trickles down each cheek. "If you take us home now, we don't need new clothes."

Though we can't see his face, I think his eyes smile.

"I know you're scared. There are many frightened children in America today. I think you can help them." He turns and leaves the room.

I let go of Bethany and walk to the door. I gently turn the handle, but the man locked the door.

I turn to see Bethany staring at me, frowning. "Your daddy makes children cry."

I am too puzzled to be angry. "My daddy's job is to help people."

She shakes her head, hard. "He takes them away from their parents. It's on TV."

Since BabyJack came, we don't keep the TV on much. Mommy says it will wake him up, and she puts in DVDs for me to watch. All my favorites.

"My daddy works for the president. The president's job is to help people."

Bethany stands straighter. "He only helps white people. He wants Spanish people to go back to their countries."

"That's not true! President Diamond is making America great again!"

Bethany stares at me. "You don't know anything."

I shout, "I know lots. My daddy…"

The voice from the other side of the door is firm. "Girls."

We both stand still. We don't want the ropes.

"You need to be quieter. And don't fight. It won't help you." He walks away from the door.

We stare at each other, and Bethany's eyes go to the bed. "I want some apple juice."

In a small voice, I say, "Me, too." I look at the bed. "We can take turns reading Harry Potter."

Bethany whispers, "We need a magic wand."

CHAPTER THIRTEEN
THE JEFE

Saturday, early evening, Maryland, near DC

The president himself calls at five PM. "We're going to find your daughter. The FBI, I don't always like them, but they do kidnappings good. We'll find your daughter and there will be a big, beautiful reunion. The girls can visit the White House. You can come with them."

I gulp. "Thank you, Mr. President. I've heard...do you think these people took my daughter, the girls, because I did the press conference on the child protection removals?"

On his end, I can hear a man talking quietly, apparently advising him.

The president speaks again. "These people, if they say that, they're Democrats who want to make me look bad. A big beautiful reunion, I'm telling you." When I can think of nothing to say, he adds, "My people will be in constant touch. Constant touch." He hangs up.

Agent Saldano says, "He means well."

Is she being sarcastic? I can't tell.

My wife speaks from the doorway. "No, he doesn't care at all." She gives me a hard stare. "This is your fault. They took her because of those kids being separated…"

She puts her face in her hands and sobs, and I jump up to go to her. Without looking up, she keeps one hand over her face and holds the other at an arm's length from her. "No!"

I stop a few feet from her. "We'll get her, them, back."

She removes the hand from her face and drops both arms to her sides as she studies the FBI agents. "I trust the FBI. Find our daughter." She turns and leaves the living room.

Agent Saldano gestures to the couch, where she still sits. "Have a seat, Mr. Delaney. Would you like some coffee? One of the agents made a pot in the kitchen."

I shake my head, but sit.

She smiles. "Maria. You can call me Maria."

The phone of the agent I knew to be called Frederick Schubert buzzes, and he studies a message. Then he smiles. "We think we have contact. That's always good." His smile fades. "But, uh, they do tie it to the border separations."

I swallow. "How so?"

"They say they will, uh, release the girls when the family separations stop."

My stomach clenches. I take a breath. I don't want to throw up. Instead, I stand. "I know the attorney general will talk to me. Can you reach him?"

While Agent Schubert talks quietly on his phone across the room, I walk from one side of the living room to the other. A glance from my side of the blinds shows my across-the-street neighbor talking to a woman I didn't know. For a few minutes, a news van had been in front of the house, but the FBI made them move to the end of the block. Maybe the woman I don't recognize is a reporter. What is our neighbor saying about our family?

How could a van have gotten in and out of the neighborhood without anyone noting even a license plate? But why would they? A woman walking her dogs remembered only a blue, late model van, not even the color of a plate.

A tap on my shoulder makes me jerk my head sharply.

"Sorry, sir, a call from your office." The agent hands me the phone and walks back to the dining room.

"Joe? It's Sarah. I came down to the office."

"Have you heard anything? Supposedly they were kidnapped because…"

She almost hisses. "Joe, you haven't said that to anyone in the press, have you?"

"No, I haven't talked to anyone like that."

She sighs. "That's good. McKenzie is handling the media. Leave it to him."

"McKenzie? Doesn't the FBI give updates or something?"

"I suppose on the girls. I'm talking about the fake news about the kidnapping being about separating families."

From the entry to the dining room, an agent waves his arms and mouths, "No."

I'd forgotten they were monitoring all calls. Apparently I am not supposed to mention the demand.

"Fake news?" I ask.

"Rumors," she says. "We have to stay on message. Let the FBI find your daughter, and her friend, of course."

I can't believe Sarah's concern is on immigration policies rather than Kyra. "I, uh, won't talk to the media. But I thought, maybe, the attorney general could at least announce something. Even if it's only a short-term change."

"Joe, don't make this about politics. Just concentrate on your daughter."

"I am *only* concentrating on my daughter!"

"I'll keep you posted on what's going on down here." Sarah hangs up.

I take the phone away from my ear and stare at it. The administration doesn't give a crap about my family. We are on our own.

CHAPTER FOURTEEN
THE REPORTER

Saturday, east of El Paso, Texas

Saturday afternoon, Juan and I decide I will approach the Border Patrol to find out where the woman and children were taken, whether they are together. The agency has offered no official comment on today's photos on the website. When the print edition is out, there will be an even larger barrage of negative comments. I am counting on the Border Patrol wanting to at least talk to me off the record.

I am wrong. But I persist. With half-a-dozen Border Patrol locations in and around El Paso, I will never find the agents who took the woman and her children. But because of the photos, people are probably talking about them.

Juan and I head to one of the locations on the eastern side of the city, since that's where he took the pictures. The El Paso Ysleta Port of Entry sits in an industrial area. Not exactly neighborhood bars for agents to hang out in.

I glance at a sign. "There's a Cesar Chavez Border Highway?"

Juan grunts. "Makes people feel welcome. Get on it, and I'll show you where to get off near a sporting complex. Couple bars near there with big-screen TVs."

I do as directed. The El Grande Sports Bar looks shabby from the outside, but the booths and tables seem new, and they sell huge burgers. "Good choice. Food's on me."

Juan grins. "Ok, Mr. Expense Account."

I like him. He's young, hungry, and passionate.

I glance around the large room. It seems half the conversations are in Spanish, half in English. I peg a group of four men at the bar as possibly agents. Two have the bulge of guns on their hip. Almost normal in Texas, but they look too clean-cut to be rowdies. They sure know how to pack away the beer.

In a low voice, I say, "Let's head for a table behind those guys."

We place our orders, and I listen intently. They speak in lowered tones, but now and then phrases like, "It's gotta end sometime," and "Tired of this shit," come through.

Finally, the youngest of the men pulls back from the bar and puts a couple of bills on it. "I didn't sign up for this. Even my kids ask about it."

I grin at Juan and put the car keys on our table. "Bingo. I'll pay, why don't you get the car open so we can hit the road when we need to." I walk to the cash register at the end of the bar and gesture for the bartender.

I collect my change in time to walk out with the fed-up agent. "Headin' home?"

He takes in my Washington Capitals tee-shirt. "You're a long way from home."

I stick out a hand. "Sam Wolfe. Following up on a story."

That stops him. "Reporter?"

"Washington Post."

"Media people are mostly in Washington. I'm not one of 'em." He continues toward his car as Juan pulls our car next to us the agent and me, and rolls down the window.

The Border Patrol guy jerks his head toward Juan. "Who are you?"

"Tour guide."

The guy stops walking and almost leers. "Funny."

Juan does a friendly smile routine. "Serious. The gringo doesn't know his way around down here."

"I'm following up on those photos on the *Post's* website this morning. The mother and two little kids."

He faces me. "I know what you mean. I wasn't there. Don't know who was."

"Do you know if they stayed together?"

He stares at me for several seconds. "Hear the mother was taken to El Paso General. You didn't hear it from me." He walks toward a car without looking back, gets in, and drives away.

I slide in the front seat of the rental car, baffled. "I can't believe he told us that."

Juan steers us into traffic. "Wasn't he the one who said he didn't sign up for this, whatever 'this' is?"

I agree, and we drive to the hospital in silence.

CHAPTER FIFTEEN

THE COLONEL

Saturday afternoon, El Paso General Hospital, Texas

Serving in the Air Force for twenty-two years didn't give me a lot of civilian connections, but my years as a NASA civilian contractor in Houston did. The guy in the cubicle next to mine has a sister in El Paso, and she has a cousin who works for the Border Patrol. Or something like that.

My own bluster gets us the information that Isabella Sanchez is in El Paso General. No one seems to know anything about the two children, whom I assume were hers. Manuel's children, Tito's grandchildren.

My smart Annie thought of the flowers. She says you can walk almost anywhere in a hospital if you carry a bouquet and wear a concerned look. I do love that woman.

She also suggests I wear my uniform. Military etiquette says retirees generally should not wear them for anything but ceremonial purposes or to receive an award. I don't know of any military etiquette that advocates taking kids from their parents. If wearing my uniform will get me to Isabella in that hospital, so much the better.

I perspire as we sit in the lobby of El Paso General. I remember a line in *Independence Day*, from a pilot about to attack the extraterrestrial invaders. "I picked a hell of a day to stop drinking." But I say this only to myself.

I lean closer to Annie. "You have those phone numbers, right?"

She smiles. "In my purse and in my bra."

I flush. The Sanchez family didn't have a phone, even a cell phone. But I had contact numbers for them through the town office and a nearby larger grocery store. I hadn't called as much since Tito died five years ago. I wish I'd kept in better touch.

Annie's Spanish is better than mine. She was the one who learned of Manuel's murder and Isabella's flight. She and the children left in the middle of the night a month ago, so they didn't become an example for what happens when widows try to escape a gang's wrath.

I can't imagine the hardships she and the children endured as they walked north for a month.

After half-an-hour, a young Hispanic woman calls us to a small conference room in what she calls "the Executive Suite." Already seated are a perspiring middle-aged man in a U.S. Border Patrol uniform and a woman whose suit and demeanor say senior hospital official.

She stands. "Thank you for your concern about the patient, Isabella Sanchez. Captain Forman of the Border Patrol is here to explain her situation. Since she is in their custody, she is a patient we are caring for, but she is under their control."

We shake hands and introduce ourselves all around as she says this. The Border Patrol man wipes his brow as we sit. The young woman who escorted us into the room sits at the far end of the table, a notebook in front of her.

Annie says, "Thanks so much for seeing us. We're so glad Isabella is being treated here. We care about her very much, and also about the children. As you may or may not know, she and the kids were trying to get to us."

The Border Patrol captain sits up straighter. "You? Are you saying you encouraged them to enter the country illegally?"

I continue to let Annie speak for us. What the U.S. Air Force calls my mild PTSD tends to make me impatient when people try to intimidate me. Most learn not to.

Annie smiles. "Her husband and father-in-law saved my husband's life in Honduras in the early 1990s. Tito, her father-in-law, died a few years ago. You've probably already learned her husband was murdered a few weeks ago. In part for defying gang members who demanded protection money if they were to continue to operate their family grocery store."

The young Hispanic woman gasps, but Annie doesn't look at her as she continues, "But Manual Sanchez has had a target on his back for years because the family was friendly with American troops at Soto Cano Air Base. Isabella was coming here to seek asylum so she and her children didn't suffer her husband's fate."

"You should have notified us," Border Patrol Captain Francis Forman says.

"We didn't know about the murder," Annie says. "They have a standing invitation for assistance…"

Forman tries to interrupt her, but Annie doesn't stop. "…and fortunately knew to leave before she and the children were also killed." She nodded to me. "My husband is the Colonel Bill referred to in the *Washington Post* article. You probably saw the article and photos."

Forman is clearly trying to hide his anger. Annie and I know it's our earlier reference to the article, as well as my uniform, that have gotten us this far.

"There are many tragic circumstances, but that does not give this Isabella the right to enter the U.S. illegally.

I say, "She did, of course, have the right to apply for asylum, which I assume she did when you picked her up. We're happy to support her claim and take responsibility for her and the children. We assume she had no knowledge of the process, but found someone to lead them here after her husband's murder. Has she told you she worked with a coyote?"

Forman shifts in his seat. "I haven't spoken with her."

For the first time, I sense that something terrible has happened to Isabella. I smile at Forman. "If we can't see her immediately, may we speak to someone who knows her circumstances? And especially the children's location. We're prepared to take them to Houston straightaway. If Isabella can't travel today, we'll return for her."

"That's not the way it works."

I stand and raise my pant leg, showing the pale, long scar along and behind my calf. "When I was shot in Honduras, in the femoral artery, Tito Sanchez and his young son Manuel staunched the bleeding and got me to a Honduran clinic. Without them, I would have died. You can understand that we want to 'make it work' as well as possible for Isabella Sanchez and her children."

I lower my pant leg and sit, but I don't take my eyes off Forman. "Are the children nearby?"

"Because of privacy laws, I can't discuss individual custody cases."

Annie's tone becomes strident. "Privacy? The photographer heard Isabella mention Colonel Bill. Surely you can talk to the person she was so anxious to find."

The young woman at the far end of the table murmurs something I don't catch. The hospital executive sits back in her chair.

I continue. "I respect your role. As you might suspect from my uniform, I generally follow the rules. But I also believe in action over apathy. If you can't guide us to the children, I'm sure the media can."

Forman fixes first me and then Annie with a stare before he says, "As you might guess, the U.S. Border Patrol will not be bullied."

The younger hospital employee again says something low-voiced in Spanish. Annie suppresses a smile.

Annie takes over. "As the people she was trying to get to, we'd like to know Isabella's condition. We've contacted a Spanish-speaking attorney to represent her, and I know you'll be allowed to tell him."

We hadn't hired one yet, but the agent doesn't know that. We can get one in a heartbeat.

"She needs to approve a lawyer," Forman snaps.

The room becomes very still. I ask, "Are you saying she is in no condition to approve her attorney?"

Forman looks away, then stands. "I leave when we talk lawyers. You can contact the regional office in Dallas."

He leaves without even nodding at the hospital exec. When he's gone, she says, "Believe it or not, it's hard for them, too." She nods at the younger woman, who leaves the room, flashing a quick smile at Annie as she goes.

When she's gone, the executive says, "Our staff are not supposed to talk about patients, but sometimes when they can't relay information themselves, we speak to people they designate. This is…awkward at several levels."

Annie nods. She has her hands in her lap, and moves them to her knees so she can better control the shaking. "We truly aren't trying to make this hard for you. But we have to help them."

The woman pulls a piece of folded paper from her suit pocket. "Media attention and protests haven't budged this president. But maybe a call to this person will help." She hands the paper to Annie. "May I offer you coffee before you leave?"

We get the message. She wants to be kind, but the hospital can better help the patients if we don't make waves from inside the building.

We find a shady bench outside the hospital, and I dial the number.

An energetic-sounding voice says, "Sam Wolfe here."

CHAPTER SIXTEEN
COROZÓN

Children's Holding Facility, Saturday, past midnight, El Paso Sector

Pico and I are put in a room with four cots but no other children. I plan to lie on top of Pico so no one can take him. I know I will sleep hard because I am so tired.

The woman who washed us comes back into the room. She holds a small stuffed animal for Pico. It has floppy ears, but we don't have it in Honduras.

He smiles really big, and takes the animal and puts it in his mouth.

The woman frowns a little.

"He is doing the teething," I tell her.

She nods at me. "It is well after midnight. Sleep a bit. Later today you will be with other children. There are lots more toys."

"Mamá? Pico says.

The woman smiles at him and closes the door. She has left the light on. I will be able to sleep even with the light.

Children's Holding Facility, Saturday morning, El Paso Sector

When I wake up there is no Pico under me. I jump out of bed and start to run to the door. A giggle comes from under the bed we slept in. I kneel and see him covering his eyes for peek-a-boo. I motion he should crawl out. He pushes the stuffed toy ahead of him, and does as I ask.

I pick him up and put him on the bed. He rubs his tummy. Pico is hungry, too. I tell him the nice lady will bring us food.

But it is a different woman. She does not have a gun, and her uniform is different. But she does have food. Two bowls of dry cereal. We do not eat this at home, Papi had some in the store for tourists hiking near our town.

We have no table or chairs, so the woman puts it on a cot that does not have a blanket. Pico crawls to her very fast, and grabs the cot to pull himself up. It starts to topple, and the woman holds it down.

In Spanish, she says to me, "We're working on ways to make the cots more stable."

I st**are at her, and slowly approach the food. Pico sticks his hand in one bowl and stuffs dry cereal in his mouth.

The woman holds up a small bottle of milk. I know it to be the cold kind tourists like. Pico and I drink warm milk from our goat. But our goat is gone, sold with everything we could not carry on the long walk to America. I feel the tears and blink very fast.

I let the woman pour milk on my cereal, and she takes a plastic spoon from her pocket and hands it to me. Then she sits on another cot and talks to me as we eat.

"Today we will help you take a shower and give you more clean clothes. Then you will play with other kids your age."

I am only ten, but Mamá has always said I am very smart. "Pico is not my age. Pico stays with me."

The woman is about Mamá's age. I wonder if she has children.

She sits up straighter. "Pico will play with different children. He will also have clean clothes and…"

I talk louder. "Pico stays with me until Mamá is here to get us."

Pico says, "Mamá?"

She smiles. "Pico wears a diaper, so he plays with other children who do. We have more helpers in that room, to change diapers."

"I change Pico's diaper." This is true, but usually Mamá changes it. Then she rinses it in the creek and puts on his other diaper. Last night the nice woman gave Pico a paper diaper. I have seen these many times. They are *basura* after the baby uses them.

The woman stands. "Please finish your cereal so I can help you clean up. Would you like to wash your hair?"

I would, but I move closer to Pico.

I carry Pico when we leave the room. He wants to crawl, but I hold him tight. For the first time, I hear the voices of other children.

The woman we have today walks with us toward a bathroom for me to use, and then we will have showers. I have only had baths, but I don't tell her I don't want the water coming down on me.

We stop outside the bathroom and she talks to another woman, but in English. Very fast. I can tell they argue. Finally, I say, "May I please go to the toilet?"

Both women switch to Spanish and the one who gave us cereal tries to take Pico from me. I tell her, "Pico can sit on the floor."

I carry Pico into the biggest bathroom I have ever seen. It is the largest and the first one with bars on the windows.

There are rows of doors, and I hear a toilet flush. A girl comes out of one of the doors and smiles at me. She is older, but she also has black hair, and it is very curly.

Now I have to go very badly. I carry Pico into the tiny space that has only a toilet. We had a *letrina* behind or house, but I used many toilets when we walked to America. Mostly in Wal-Mart stores by the road. Mamá had to hold tight to Pico so he didn't touch everything.

Before I sit, I roll the toilet paper so Pico can play with it. He will stay with me if he plays. He grabs at the paper and tries to stuff it in his mouth. "No. Pico does not eat it." He hands it to me.

I use the toilet and take some more paper from Pico. I am very scared. I think they will try to take Pico from me when we go outside the bathroom.

I wash my hands and pick up Pico. When we go outside the bathroom, the two women are there. And a man who is maybe twenty years. He has two toys for Pico. One is a plastic car that he rolls on the floor.

Pico wants to wiggle down to catch the car. I can't hold him, so I put him on the floor and start to follow him. The man is faster. He lifts Pico and the toy, and laughs at Pico. Pico laughs with him.

The woman who gave us cereal says, "John will wash Pico while I help you."

I am so scared I sit on the floor. My head pounds and I feel very cold. Pico laughs. He doesn't realize I am not coming with him.

If I cry, Pico will cry. The cereal woman stoops in front of me. "John will play with your Pico."

John turns a corner, and I hear Pico's first cry. He is afraid. I put my head on my knees and cry very, very hard.

CHAPTER SEVENTEEN
KYRA

Saturday evening, somewhere near DC

I don't like it here, but I am not afraid. When Bethany cried, a man brought us ice cream. I don't think people who plan to kill you bring you ice cream. He says we can talk to our parents, but just for a moment, so they know we're okay. But not just yet.

Bethany is a year older than I am, and she watches television a lot. She says we should try to stay on the phone a long time because then the police can find us.

I am not sure about this. I want to be home, but I don't want the ropes. If we talk a long time, maybe the man will put the ropes on us.

Now we have only the one man, the one who brings us food. Sometimes I put my ear near the bottom of the door and can hear him talking to someone, but I'm pretty sure he talks on a phone. No one answers him.

I lie on the floor to read the books. Except for the Harry Potter book, they are for first-graders. But I read them because I am so very bored. I wish the window wasn't so high up. Today, instead of only blue sky, clouds pass. Sometimes a lot, and we have sun and shadows.

The man knocks and Bethany and I stare at the door.

"I'm coming in. Stand back." He enters with a tray with cut-up apples and cheese sandwiches with mustard.

Bethany and I don't like mustard. When he brought us sandwiches the first time, we scraped it off with toilet paper from the bathroom and flushed it.

He puts the tray on the bed. "After you eat, I'm going to record your voices to send to your parents as a message. You can say you're okay and..."

Bethany's tears start again. "You said we could talk to them."

"Change of plans. You don't have to, it can be only Kyra recording. But I think your parents want to hear your voice." He leaves.

I try to turn the doorknob again. Maybe one time he will forget to lock it. Not this time.

Bethany puts her head on the pillow and cries into it. I take the sandwiches to the bathroom to wipe off the mustard.

I will eat quickly so I can record my message. If I'm a good girl, maybe it will help us go home soon.

CHAPTER EIGHTEEN
THE JEFE

Saturday night, Maryland, near DC

I'm used to taking charge, to always being able to answer questions from my staff, from campaign volunteers, and especially Kyra. Now, all I can do is ask.

Ask and watch the TV news. The FBI agents want me to watch it less, but I feel my connection to Kyra is stronger when her picture flashes on CNN or Fox News.

Even the Fake News *Washington Post* has a large story on the same page as the story about the two kids sitting on the desert floor clutching each other. At least their mother is with them.

My wife barely speaks to me. She thinks Kyra was kidnapped because, as she puts it, I'm "one of the key faces of the abhorrent practice of separating parents and children."

My own wife. I put her words out of my mind. I can only focus on Kyra.

An FBI agent I don't know rushes into our living room and holds his phone to the agent in charge. He puts it to his ear, listens, and smiles.

"Come listen to this, Mr. Delaney. We have proof of life."

Kyra's voice is calm. "I'm okay, Mommy and Daddy. I want to come home, but no one is hurting me. Or Bethany. I love you."

Jubilation wells inside me. "So, you can trace the call, right? Find out where…"

The agent in charge shakes his head. "It was a recording sent via message to my secretary's phone. God knows how they got her number."

Angela rushes into the living room. "Let me hear, I need to hear her!"

Agent Saldano follows with a crying BabyJack, holding his bottle. She must have been feeding him, or maybe Angela was and the agent took him.

Angela listens, then looks at the agent in charge. "So you'll use this to find her, right?"

"Have a seat, Mrs. Delaney."

"I'm not some vixen about to faint. You can use this to find her, can't you?"

"We've already determined it's a throw-away phone. But we can possibly locate the area from which the text was sent."

He had been holding the phone loosely. Angela grabs it and hurls it at the picture window, splintering the phone and cracking the window. "You've already determined! How long have you had my little girl's voice?"

Stunned silence follows her throw. Slowly the agent in charge reaches down to pick up his phone. "Mrs. Delaney, we had it less than an hour. Our first priority was trying to trace the message."

Angela looks at the window, then at her empty hand. She looked as shocked as I feel. She sinks to the floor and puts her head on her knees. Her sobs are loud and almost violent. "My God. They have my little girl. Where have they taken her?"

CHAPTER NINETEEN
THE REPORTER

Saturday, early evening, near El Paso, Texas

I'm excited and gesture to Juan to pull over. He takes an off-ramp from Interstate 10 and drives toward a gas station as I listen.

"I was given this number," a man's voice says. "May I ask to whom I'm speaking?"

"This is Sam Wolfe, of the *Washington Post*."

When the man says who he is, I grin.

"Who is it?" Juan asks.

I cover the mouthpiece part of my call phone. "Colonel Bill." I push the button for the phone's speaker.

"You wrote the story and published the pictures of Manuel's wife, Isabella, and the children."

"The *Post* published it, yes. My name is the byline, but much of the story comes from a freelancer, Juan Gomez. He took the photos."

Juan leans toward the phone. "This is Juan. Good to meet you, Mr. Colonel."

"Bill. Bill Haines. My wife, Annie, and I drove to El Paso. We want to find them. Do you know where the Border Patrol took the children?"

My mind races. Does he have Isabella with him? "No. A source told us Isabella is in El Paso General, but…"

"We were just there," Bill says. "Someone there gave me your number." His tone becomes urgent. "But you can't print that. That we were given your number."

"No problem. We're very careful."

"Isabella is in the hospital, but we think she may be badly hurt. It seems she can't talk. We don't know where the children are."

"We've been looking, too. We're not far from central El Paso. Where are you?"

"In front of the hospital."

I look at Juan. "You know where it is?"

"We're twenty minutes out," Juan says. "We're in a white Ford Focus rental car. You want to wait in front for us, or go somewhere else?"

Bill talks to a woman, and then says, "My wife says she can see a Starbucks at a corner, kind of across and east of the main hospital entrance."

I glance at my phone. "I can see your number. Can you give me your wife's, in case we have trouble finding you?"

He does. "I'd like to ask you a couple more questions while we drive, then I'll let you get to Starbucks, is that okay?"

It is, and Bill tells me, in bullet-point precision, about Manuel and his father, Tito, saving his life in Honduras many years ago. His voice momentarily breaks when he says he didn't know about Manuel's death, though from what he and his wife have pieced together, it happened shortly before Isabella took the kids and left for the United States. Beyond that, he knows nothing of their trip or capture.

We disconnect. I could ask twenty more questions as we drive, but Juan and I need to plan our next steps. We discuss whether we simply report, or if we should get involved.

Juan turns on the radio, and we hear the sound of children crying in the camps.

Juan's eyes stay on the road. "I say we get involved."

I agree.

CHAPTER TWENTY
THE COLONEL

Saturday, early evening, El Paso

Annie and I have ordered four iced teas. We figure the reporters will be thirsty, too. I reach for her hand across the table. "How attached are you to my pension?"

She laughs, the first time that day. "I'm willing to work at Wal-Mart if we can get those kids." Her smile fades. "And Isabella, of course."

"Do you have one of those cards you make grocery lists on?"

"A three-by-five card. Of course." She pulls out a bright yellow one.

I take it and pull a pen from the breast pocket of my short-sleeved shirt. "We need a plan."

"A plan?"

"So we know how far we're willing to go with this." My list starts with media interaction. After I write it, I look at her.

She nods slowly. "I pretty much trust the police not to hurt us, so I'm willing to protest. Even...even tie myself to a Border Patrol fence."

I shake my head emphatically. "Then it's the president's people who haul us out of there. If it comes to that, I think we're safer with local cops than feds."

She stares at me for a second, and her face crumples in tears.

"God, Annie, I'm sorry."

She grabs a brown napkin and fiercely blots each eye. A woman at the table next to us asks, in Spanish-accented English, "Is she okay?"

"Yes," I say. "We're trying to find some friends."

A young boy and girl with her, he about six, she four, exchange glances. The woman says, "We are, too."

I want to see if they mean what we mean, but I turn back to Annie.

She blows her nose. "I can't believe it's come to this. In America, we're trying to decide which kinds of police are better."

The woman says, "ICE, they are not police." She looks at the kids with her. "Remember, police you can call, never talk to ICE."

Annie realizes she has probably frightened the children. "We're sad because a friend was hurt, and we can't find her children. We want to help them."

The woman, whose careworn face tells me she's about forty, says, "Border Patrol? They don't want to take the kids."

I wonder how she knows this. I look from Annie to the woman, and take a chance. "We're trying to decide how far we should go to try to get the family. They were coming to us to get help with asylum."

In Spanish, the little girls asks the woman where we are going, and if they should go, too.

We three adults smile, and the woman looks at the children and says, in English, "They are not sure what to do, either." To us, she says, "My name is Alicia. You can make more choices. I have a green card, but I'm not yet a citizen."

The door opens, and two men enter and scan the room. Few people are in the Starbucks, so when they see us, they smile and walk over. The white man says, "The Haines, I presume."

I stand, Annie stays seated, and the men join our table. I nod at Alicia. I won't repeat what she said, but I do say, "These are reporters. We hope they can help us."

Alicia does not introduce herself, but she smiles. She picks up her ice water and a box of juice the kids were sharing. "We have an appointment. I wish you luck, too."

Juan and Sam go to the counter to order coffee. When they return, I explain our conversation with Alicia. When Juan seems interested enough to follow her, I say, "I think she wants to be left alone."

Both men nod, and Sam says, "So we know Isabella is there, and perhaps not in great shape. I called my editor a few minutes ago. He's got someone working the phones to see what we can find out about the kids. Sadly, they probably aren't together anymore."

CHAPTER TWENTY-ONE
COROZÓN

Children's Holding Center, Saturday morning and afternoon, El Paso Sector

I didn't hear Pico cry for very long, because I think they carried him out of the building. The women let me cry, and then one of them put a hand under my elbow. In Spanish, she says, "Stand up, honey."

I know she did not learn Spanish at home, or she would call me *mi hija*. "Where is my Pico going?"

"Someplace safe."

With her help, I stand. "He is safe with me. Only Mamá and me! Where is Mamá?"

"We're going back to the room where you slept last night. We put coloring books and juice in there for you. Later, we're going to take you to a big room with some other girls. You can play with them, and then you'll have lunch. Do you like to color?"

I stamp my foot. "I need to go with Pico!"

She frowns, and the other woman says, "Stop coddling her."

The nice woman says, "If you behave, it will be okay."

I wipe my cheeks with the back of my hand. Mamá said if we stayed in our town the bad men will kill us. Now the American bad men have Mamá, and I don't know where Pico is.

When we get to the room, Pico's toy with the floppy ears is on the bed. I pick it up and put my face in its softness and cry. I don't feel brave anymore.

One of the women tells me it will be okay. She shuts the door and leaves me alone.

I see the box of crayons and large books with pictures of crayons on them. When I open the book, I understand what the crayons were for. At my school, we sometimes drew pictures, but we had no books like this.

At the back of the book is a page with no drawings on it. I start to draw a picture of Tienda Sanchez. I know every inch of our store. But it is not our store now.

I am soon tired and decide to lie on the cot where Pico and I slept. Mamá says to sleep when you can. You never know when you will have to walk far.

I wake up when two women come into the room. The one I call the nice one picks up Pico's toy and hands it to me. I thank her, because I am supposed to.

She makes a bright smile. "We'll take you to the other girls now."

When I follow the women down a long hall, I wonder if the bad men in our town would really have killed us. Then I remember the knife they put into Papi.

In my school there were many children, but even there I never saw so many girls in one place. Some are much younger than me, but none wear diapers. They do not have uniforms, like at my school, but a lot of the clothes look almost the same, only in different colors.

The nice woman walks with me to some girls who look about my age. "Girls, this is Corozón. She is new today. Can you show her around?"

They smile and say yes. I think they are the smiles my friend Marta and I sometimes gave to our teacher, and then we whispered anyway.

When the woman leaves, the girls stop smiling. The tallest one asks, "Why did you get the special treatment?"

I don't understand, so I say nothing. A girl my height looks behind her, and then shoves me with her shoulder. "Answer her!"

I swallow. "I don't know what the special treatment is."

They all stare at me. The tallest one says, "You came late, and they put you in the sick room. Are you sick?"

I shake my head. "I am only sad."

In English, one girl says, "There's a lotta that goin' around."

They all laugh.

I cannot make my lips smile. "Do you know where they take my Pico?"

The shortest girl, who has said nothing, asks, "You came with other kids?"

I nod. I can't speak.

The tall girl somehow looks kinder. "They take the babies somewhere else. And the boys."

Two more girls come to us, walking very fast. The one with straight black hair says, "She's the one from the watch! With the baby."

I don't know what she is watching, but suddenly they are all looking at me. No one says anything until the one of the new girls says, "You cannot tell anyone this. Promise."

I nod. "I promise."

"We can't have Internet or phones, but Lucinda hid her Apple watch. We see the news some."

"But not a lot, because she doesn't have a charger," the other new girl says.

I have heard of the Internet, and certainly know an apple and a watch.

"So," the tallest girl asks, "were you hugging a baby tight in the desert last night?"

I smile, very big, and look at the new girls. "Do you know where my Pico is? He came here with me, but the man took him away today."

They shake their heads, and suddenly I think they believe I am not a special treatment girl. I am like them.

We are all sad.

CHAPTER TWENTY-TWO
KYRA

Sunday morning, somewhere near DC

We still have only the one man. When he comes back to get our breakfast dishes, I ask him if we can go home today.

He shakes his head, and his eyes don't smile. "It's kind of up to what your daddy and the president do. It doesn't look as if they are ready to cooperate."

Bethany is so angry she jumps up and down. "My daddy didn't do anything bad! I want to go home." She opens her mouth to scream.

The man gets to her very fast. He puts his hand over her mouth and swings her so he is behind her. "You have to be quiet!"

I don't want the ropes. I run into the bathroom and get in the tub and pull the shower curtain shut.

It has lines in it, like it's brand new. I can hear the man talking very quietly to Bethany, but not what he is saying.

After he talks more, he calls out to me. "Kyra. You can come back out. Bethany will be quiet now."

When I come out, Bethany is sitting on the bed. She is not crying, but she looks at the floor and doesn't say anything.

"Kyra, sit next to Bethany. I want to talk to both of you."

I sit. I am very mad at Bethany. My daddy is not bad, and I don't want the ropes.

The man sits on the floor with his legs crossed, and he looks up at us. "I'm sorry you have to be here. You're scared and your parents are scared. In the United States now, lots of mommies and daddies have had their kids taken away. They're frightened, and their kids are more terrified."

I see perspiration on the man's neck. His mask must be hot.

"We think if your parents talk to the president, maybe he will let the boys and girls at the border be with their parents. It is..." He stops. "It is evil to keep them apart."

Bethany sits up straighter and frowns.

He continues, "Kyra's daddy is not evil. When he took the job with President Diamond, he didn't think he would be the person who talked to TV about the president separating parents from their children."

I think he can tell we don't know exactly what he means.

He looked from Bethany to me. "Kyra's daddy did a press conference that said it was okay to take immigrants' kids away from their parents. He may not think it is, but he needs to have a job so Kyra and her family have a house and food. Now, I heard that when we, uh, picked you up, you had been to a birthday party."

Was he telling us he wasn't in the van?

We both nod.

"So you are friends. This is a very tough time for you. But no one will hurt you. You will go home, I'm pretty sure in the next couple of days. Please don't fight. It will make it worse."

He stands.

I feel braver. "Can we have more books?"

"Books not for babies," Bethany says.

This time, I can see his lips smile, through his mask.

"I've asked, uh, some people if they will bring a TV and DVD player for you."

Bethany and I both smile. We tell him our favorite movies.

CHAPTER TWENTY-THREE
THE JEFE

Sunday morning, Maryland, near DC

The attorney general has finally agreed to talk to me. I can't believe it's taken this long. He met Kyra and Angela at his holiday staff open house. He has told me I'm an important part of what he calls his policy team.

"Mr. Attorney General. Thank you for calling me."

"Joe, I cannot tell you how saddened I am at this heinous kidnapping. The FBI director tells me he has almost fifty agents working to find your girl and her friend. I have every confidence they will succeed."

"Mr. Attorney General, in a staff meeting, you once told all of your office directors that you wanted us to tell you what we thought even if we don't agree with you."

He was silent for several seconds. "I do not recall. But, of course, I value all opinions."

"Sir, it's wrong to take those children from their parents. They took Kyra so I'd know how it feels. It's…I don't even know the words to tell you how Angela and I feel. We're…"

"Joe, Joe. The best thing for us to do is find your daughter and her friend, little, Barbie, is it?"

"Bethany. But they can do it again…"

"I have ordered the director of the FBI to do security reviews for families of our employees who work on this project. They will be advised on…"

I feel my head pound. "Project! Sir, we are taking children, babies from their parents…"

"Joe, you're upset. I understand that. But we need a deterrent. We probably feed them better than their parents did. This is short-term, just until Congress acts. The president is convinced that once we have that wall…"

"Sir, this is something the president can stop with a stroke of the pen, not some policy foisted on him by Democrats." My voice rises. "He can stop this."

"Of course he can, Joe, but you have to remember, Congress will not act unless they think their elections are in danger. We need to protect our soil. We cannot let these...people beg to be let in because they have some problems at home."

"Sir, this isn't some remote policy discussion. It's my daughter!"

"Joe, I know you face severe stress. But you need to let go of this idea. The policy stays in place."

I begin to cry in huge, gulping sobs. An FBI agent rushes to me and takes the phone from my hand. Angela almost runs to me and puts her hand on my shoulder. We sit on the floor together, sobbing.

The FBI agent speaks into the phone. "We will assist Mr. and Mrs. Delaney, sir."

Through my sobs I can hear the attorney general's distinctive drawl. "Please do give them both my best regards." He hangs up.

Angela and I cling to one another, the first time we have really been able to comfort each other. I kiss the top of her head.

Then I stop sobbing and pull back. Surprised at my abrupt change, Angela sobs the word, "What?"

"He said it's the president's policy, not something he's required by law to do. They want to keep persecuted people from seeking asylum."

The agent who took the phone stands very still.

Agent Saldano smiles as she burps BabyJack.

By noon, I have a plan. I can't very well walk out to the news trucks and state my 200 percent change of heart, much less the attorney general's statement that he wants to frighten asylum seekers, that the kids are pawns in a sick game of deterrence.

I can try to get to the media, but the FBI can block me, and I wouldn't be able to get two sentences out without breaking down. If I do this, I'll never work in Washington again, but at this point that is far down my list of concerns.

All of us read that morning's paper. The *Washington Post* – quoting someone not authorized to share the information, of course – stated the FBI believes that Kyra and Bethany were taken so a senior administration official will understand the pain parents feel at the border. No one at the Department of Justice commented on the story.

As our story had been on the *Post's* webpage, in the print edition, our kidnappings ran next to stories about the two children Border Patrol agents tried to pry apart.

The *Post* says that the mother, who had screamed next to her children as an agent handcuffed her, is in a hospital in El Paso. They also know she's seeking asylum because of her husband's murder.

And they found Colonel Bill. Colonel Bill had a great deal to say about the treatment of those who had saved his life decades earlier.

If I can reach them, they will be powerful allies.

CHAPTER TWENTY-FOUR
THE REPORTER

Sunday afternoon, El Paso

A good reporter stays neutral. Or acts it, anyway. Leaves the editorializing to the analysts, pundits, and his own editors. Other than something like jumping in a river to save a drowning kid, we don't get involved in a story.

I was about to be involved. Very involved.

Bill Haines had penned a forceful opinion piece that appeared on the *Post's* webpage and will be in the paper's Monday print edition. Not being much of a keyboarder, he dictated it to me. My eyes were moist more often than his.

Without Tito and Manuel Sanchez, no Bill Haines would be here today. Two of his and Annie's three children were born after Tito and

Manuel saved his life. Both teach in elementary schools.

But, he didn't dwell on himself. He described Honduras as two countries. A beautiful place with peaceful people and a land of terror where drug kingpins and gangsters ruled.

Manuel Sanchez was one of their many victims, and Isabella could not wait to see if she would be next. She expected to be. She did what any sensible parent, any person, would do. She fled to what she thought was safety.

She came to the country that grants asylum to the persecuted. That protects an individual or family while their case is heard. Until now, when some do not have the chance to state their case before their entry is criminalized and their children taken from them.

Isabella's case is a powerful one, made more so by her apparent injury while in Border Patrol custody. We are being careful not to paint the Border Patrol agents as the bad guys, but people have picked up on the images Juan took.

In a legal sense, those who cannot prove their imminent danger at home, or simply come because their family is starving, have no right to be here, according to this president. That their children are taken from them is their own fault. They are criminals pure and simple, and should have stayed home and starved or huddled in the streets. As a family unit, of course.

As reporters spread out across the country, we have all found that even most immigration hardliners don't think children should be taken from their parents and essentially placed in cages. The administration tries to say they are protecting the kids from some danger and the kids are well-treated.

They are certainly fed and have clothes, but anyone who keeps a dog in the backyard knows a cage when they see one, even if the enclosures are meant to be transitory before the kids get to their tents and porta potties.

With Bill and Annie Haines, Juan Gomez and I are organizing a protest outside El Paso General Hospital. We have no permits for a Sunday evening display of outrage. But in a matter of hours, we have hundreds of people indicating, on Facebook of course, that they will participate.

I expect to be fired on Monday, but it will be a helluva story.

Annie has spent the day lining up food trucks, and she bought dozens of cases of water. They weigh down her car and mine. (Juan's rust bucket not being able to play a part in any demonstration.)

Several times I have heard Annie tell Bill to be careful or slow down, and he perspires a lot. He seems to have the energy of a twenty-year old, so while I'm keeping an eye on him, I can't worry about him.

We are setting up in front of the hospital largely because sources tell us Isabella is still there, and because this main entrance is across from a huge city park. Hundreds already sit in the park and a few throw Frisbees. All allowed on a Sunday afternoon.

Several El Paso police cruisers park at the park edges, but so far, no one has come to tell us to leave. And how could they eject a crowd streaming from so many directions?

My editor calls. "Okay, CNN has video of you and the colonel front and center. I don't suppose I need to tell you a reporter is not part of the story."

I think I hear humor in his voice. "You don't. And I'm sorry, because it will give the mor...man in the White House a basis to say the *Washington Post* is biased against him."

"We can only report on his policies and how they affect people. I'll probably have to suspend you."

"I was figuring you'd fire me."

"Hell no. You'd get some talking head job that pays more than I earn."

I use our tag line. "Democracy Dies in Darkness."

"I called for some real substance. We got an email forwarded from a lady who got it from she won't say who. But it looks like the little girl, the Sanchez girl."

"What? Where? Is she where Bill and Annie can get her? What about the little boy?"

"I don't know a lot, but from the background, it's kind of grainy, it looks like a big cafeteria. We've shared it with every outlet. Somebody'll recognize the spot. If that woman is hurt, her kids deserve to be with her."

I stop setting up the public address systems I've been working on. "We talk about her a lot. You know Border Patrol wouldn't keep her in there if they could move her."

"You got any leads?"

"Hospital staff are tight-lipped. Privacy and all that."

"Somebody'll talk. Good luck this afternoon. And I didn't say that."

CHAPTER TWENTY-FIVE
THE COLONEL

Sunday, late afternoon, El Paso

It's coming together. We have three speakers – me, a retired Border Patrol agent, and a woman who runs a youth shelter in Houston, a friend of Annie's. She's flying in on a private plane owned by an oil multi-millionaire. The president has galvanized even the nation's richest citizens against him.

I send prayers skyward so the event stays peaceful. It's only for two hours, five to seven PM, and it's hot as hell. That should encourage people to leave.

I've talked to hospital brass a couple of times. I tell them we will keep people in the park. I hope my uniform helps do that, but in reality it can't. People have to buy into peaceful protest.

At four-thirty-five, a line of half-a-dozen buses pulls alongside the park and men and women disembark. I can't read their signs yet. Then someone unfurls a banner. "Military Veterans for Kids." Easily three-quarters wear their uniforms.

I sit down on our hastily assembled stage. I want to cry. It's going to be okay.

In a couple of minutes, five people who look like America walk up to me. A white guy in biker gear with a long grey pony tail, a younger black guy in a dress Marine uniform, an Asian woman in an Air Force uniform, an Hispanic woman in Army combat gear, and a white woman in Navy whites.

The biker grins and speaks first. "You need to get this show on the road. These guys'll pass out, wearing those uniforms."

They all want to shake my hand. I tell them everyone helping deserves a handshake, but we're out of time. After we agree that they will all stand on stage and speak briefly, I put them to work on crowd control.

Sam Wolfe and Juan Gomez are in the crowd telling people the format – it's not like we had time to prepare a program. Annie has set up a small red tent with a few medical supplies, including a defibrillator that set me back $1,100 via Amazon one-day delivery.

As the tent's purpose becomes known, men and women from throughout the crowd walk over. I assume medical professionals willing to volunteer. Our big concern is children getting overheated.

At four-fifty PM, Juan Gomez and the biker vet do a sound check. Then a family carrying a large duffel bag rushes the stage. For two seconds I'm afraid they have weapons, but they open it and pull out dozens of mini American flags. They begin attaching them to our stage with grey duct tape. In a minute twenty people are helping them and an equal number of photographers record and snap pictures.

At five PM, I take the stage with our three anticipated speakers and the five military veterans. After weeks of shame, I have never been so proud of my country. I introduce them and gesture to Annie and her crew at the first-aid tent.

"My wife, Annie, who has guided us toward this rally. We will not stop until the children and parents are reunited."

I had asked Sam and Juan to join us, but they say they will accomplish more by recording and writing. I agree, and will find a way to give them credit.

Before introducing the speakers, I scan the crowd of perhaps 5,000, most of whom are seated on blankets. I ask the children to stand and lead us in the national anthem. I want to be sure the nation sees these people as the true patriots.

I tell the story of my rescue in Honduras, putting emphasis on Tito and Manuel, and describe his murder because he would not capitulate to local gangs. As hard as that is to describe, talking about Isabella's bravery in leading the children here to apply for asylum is much harder.

I ask if anyone in the audience thinks they can walk for a month through the heat with two small children. The response is a resounding no.

Then we show our one audio visual tool, the photo of the children that Juan took. Corozón's terror is the most clear. We have only two large-screen TVs, both near the front. Juan had made two hundred copies to spread among what we expected would be a far smaller crowd. Most have already seen it. A bunch of kids start to cry. I hadn't expected that.

I turn the podium over to the retired Border Patrol agent, introducing him as the voice of agents who love their own families and don't want to seize the children. He tells the crowd I have stolen his thunder, because that is his message.

He says he spent a career supporting the laws of our nation, and the Border Patrol agents treat people with respect. "And the president might be surprised to know the vast number of people crossing the border illegally treat us the same way."

A few people applaud, and more join them.

When the applause ends, he continues. "I believe that if President Diamond had to take one screaming child from a parent, he would not have the strength to stand up for his own policies." The audience cheers for two minutes.

Annie's friend who runs the youth shelter speaks for ten minutes. Her small shelter has none of the 2,300 children seized from their parents, but she has spoken to many colleagues who do house them. She stresses that the few social workers and many federal employees and contractors are doing their best to comfort the children. But no one can truly console a child who walked hundreds of miles in dire straits only to be seized by men and women in uniforms who haul them to barren facilities.

Shouts of rage and insults about many presidential qualities fill the air. Some of the signs the protestors carry are simple: Keep Families Together; Stop Seizing Children.

Others directly insult the president, the most polite of which was "Who's the animal now, Mr. Diamond?"

Two of the five military veterans have spoken when I notice two police officers escorting a woman in a nurse's uniform, accompanied by the hospital official who spoke to Annie and me only two days ago.

I climb off the stage and walk behind it to get to the two women. In a low voice, I ask, "What's up, ladies?"

The nurse appears to have been crying. "We have some sad news."

The executive asks, "Will it be appropriate to announce, here, the death of Isabella Sanchez?"

Dizziness sweeps over me, and the nurse touches my arm. "Sir?"

I straighten fully. "How, how did she die?"

"Organ failure. We just couldn't keep up..." The executive drew a breath. "She seemed to have had a seizure, which is why they brought her here. Severe dehydration, then she vomited a great deal after they took her children. The, uh, agents didn't initially realize the severity of her condition."

"Had she been," I searched for a neutral word, "injured during her capture?"

Both women shook their heads. The nurse says, "She was weak from her long journey. Then the severe dehydration, combined with the shock, physical and mental, of losing her children. In someone in your or my condition, it would have been an ordeal. For her, it was fatal."

"We failed her," I say. I glance at the stage. The fourth veteran is stressing that he fought for the rights of all people, not so that rich men can subjugate poor people fleeing oppression.

"I appreciate that you have come. I'm trying to decide how the crowd will react to the news. I don't want this to turn ugly, or…"

"It's already ugly," the executive says. "But I take your point. Angry people could cause others to be hurt."

The fifth veteran has begun to speak. I have to make a decision. "What if you say you have been caring for her, and ask for prayers for Mrs. Sanchez and her family? You can be interviewed immediately after, and announce her death. Does that feel dishonest to you?"

The nurse says, "It does, but you're right, a lot of children are here. We want to protect kids, not do something that could lead to them being hurt."

Sam Wolfe comes toward us. I gesture that he should join us. "Sam, you'll want to talk to these women as soon as they finish speaking. Maybe you and Juan can guide them through the media frenzy."

He raises his eyebrows at me.

"It's big," I say, "but we've decided that they'll simply ask for prayers for Isabella, so the crowd doesn't erupt."

"Crap," Sam says. He turns to them. "Bill has to get back on stage. I'll stand next to it with you, while you wait."

"It'll just be a few minutes," I say.

My feet are heavy as I walk behind the stage again. The joy I felt at the support of so many has evaporated. How can Annie and I get custody of the two kids? Will they hear about their mother's death on the news?

CHAPTER TWENTY-SIX
COROZÓN

Children's Holding Center, Monday morning, El Paso Sector

I am very glad the girl named Lucinda has her special watch. She can only look at it in the bathroom, where the adults watching us do not see.

Most of what she says is confusing, because I do not know about the social media or CNN. The best news is that Colonel Bill is looking for us. Yesterday he brought many people together to pray for Mamá and Pico and me. I know he will find us.

Lucinda tells us thousands of people want to find us, and I can almost not talk. I only want to find Pico and Mamá. But if many people can help look, that is good.

After breakfast, Lucinda is very quiet. I ask her if her watch says if the people looking have found Pico, but she just shakes her head. She says her watch battery is almost dead, so she doesn't think she can get more news.

The girl who shoved me yesterday is very nice. We have warm cornbread for breakfast, and she gives me some of her butter.

I spend some of the morning with a little girl who will only lie on the floor and cry. I lie next to her, like I do with Pico when he is sad. She knows I am there, but I don't ask her questions. After a while, she reaches over to touch my nose.

The tall girl brings her a book to read. It is in English, but the pictures are pretty. Just before lunch, the little girl sits on her lap. I am comforted. Maybe Pico is sitting on someone's lap. He can drool on them.

When I see him, I will give him his stuffed toy with the floppy ears. The tall girl says it is an elephant. When I say we have none in our town, she laughs and says we probably have none in all of Honduras.

The ladies who help us come to say lunch is in thirty minutes, so we should take turns washing our hands. I am in line to do that when the nice woman from yesterday finds me.

She smiles very much. "Good morning, Corozón. You are making friends."

I look at the tall girl. The little girl holds her hand. They smile at me, but then the tall girl looks away.

"The other girls help me." I almost say they want to find Pico, too, but I stop myself. I don't want the woman to know about the watch with the news.

She reaches for my hand, but I am not sure I want to take it. I don't want to be away from Mamá and Pico, but the girls here are good.

"Some people you like are here," the woman says.

I am excited. "Mamá and Pico?"

"Come see and you'll find out." She looks at my hand. "I know someone who will be glad to see the stuffed elephant."

Now I know it is Pico and Mamá, and I am so happy! Then I think of the little girl who stayed on the floor so long. "Are other mommies coming?"

The other girls walk a little closer.

"I don't know exactly when, but I think the government is going to try to find everyone's mommies and daddies." She looks at the other girls. "The people who run this shelter will tell us more. Probably tomorrow."

The woman looks as if she is nervous, so I take her hand. "I will go with you now." I smile at the other girls. "Thank you for being my friends."

We walk through the door that is always locked, and I think we are going back to the room where Pico and I slept. But we go into a different room. It has many fancy chairs. And Pico.

He has his head on a woman's shoulder when I walk in. He is very solemn, but he sees me and makes his squealing noise. I run to him, and the woman puts him on the floor for me to hug him.

Two nights ago, I held onto Pico. Today, he will not let me go. I sit on the floor and rock him, and tell him I love him. He still will not let go, but he does not squeeze too tight.

The woman who brought me in leaves and shuts the door. The woman who used to hold Pico sits on the floor in front of us, and so does the man. They smile at us.

I look mostly at the man. I have seen his picture, but it was when my daddy was a boy. I smile. "I think you are Colonel Bill."

"I am. And this is my wife, Annie. She did not meet Tito and your parents, but she has written them letters."

I nod. I know this. Letters with pictures of Christmas trees. "Did you find Mamá yet?" Then I remember to say thank you. "Thank you for asking people to pray for us."

They look at each other, and they seem sad. Colonel Bill says, "We didn't realize you knew."

I look toward the door, and then at them. I whisper. "The girl, in the room with the other girls. She had a watch that gave news. But you can't tell. She said you asked many people to pray for Mamá and Pico and me."

The man says, "Aha," and the woman says, "He did."

Then the lady named Annie says, "We are so glad to bring you Pico, but I'm afraid we also have some sad news."

When she tells me Mamá is in heaven with Papi, I wish the world could be over. But I have to take care of Pico, so I will stay in it.

CHAPTER TWENTY-SEVEN
KYRA

Monday afternoon and early evening, near DC

When the man tells us we can go home today, Bethany and I are very happy. But I know he does not want anyone to see his face, so I don't understand how he can drive us home.

"You're right, Kyra. My friends and I don't want people to recognize us. So I have to ask you a favor."

Bethany and I look at each other. I want to go home, but I'm not sure about a favor.

"We're going to drive you in a different van. It has special windows, so you can't see outside. You'll have to lie on the floor, under the back seat. We'll have a blanket for you to cover with, and if you are very, very good, you don't have to be tied up."

We promise we will be very good. We don't want the ropes.

He leaves and comes back in a few minutes. He has new dresses for us, and towels. He says he would like us to take a shower, so we look extra pretty for our parents. We say we would rather leave now, but he says we have to change.

I start to tell him Mommy always washes my hair, but I don't. I don't want him to help.

When we are finally ready, he explains more things. "We are going to drop you in a park, only a few miles from here. And then we'll tell your parents where to find you."

I am worried about this. I can see from the high window that it is almost dark.

"You'll be safe. You won't see me, but I'll wait nearby until I hear your parents' cars. Then I'll leave."

"Is this your house?" Bethany asks.

"No. And you can't ask me any more questions like that."

He leaves and locks the door. I am angry with Bethany for asking him the question, but we aren't supposed to fight, so I don't say so.

CHAPTER TWENTY-EIGHT
THE JEFE

Monday afternoon and evening, Maryland, near DC

Angela and I visited Bethany's parents, Hal and Jordan, on Sunday afternoon. We told the FBI we thought we could provide each other moral support, and they agreed.

Hal actually wore a coat and tie. I can barely make myself put on jeans or sweat pants. But his jacket was handy. I slipped the note into his pocket when I gave him a bear hug as we left. He knew I did it, but was smart enough to say nothing.

I wasn't sure how he could reach Sam Wolfe, but figured he would have a better chance than I would. Hal succeeded, because Sam did as I asked and texted me early Monday morning. And not from his office phone, from a throwaway phone using a phony name, also as I asked.

Though the FBI continues to monitor our phones, they don't restrict who can text me. The kidnappers could text from any phone. When Sam sends a chatty note saying he is sorry about Kyra, I say he is a childhood friend and I want to respond.

Angela fidgets with her coffee cup as I type. We planned the note together, so I could get the most info into a paragraph.

"The AG told me directly that parent-child separations are a deliberate choice to deter immigration, not a policy foisted on him and the president by some law the Democrats passed, as the president has been saying. I am willing to go on camera to say this. Pls report this. Quote me."

I press send.

My statement is on the airwaves in less than thirty minutes. The agent in charge leaves our house to consult with FBI headquarters in person. I have a feeling he will not be back.

When the attorney general calls, I ask Agent Saldano to tell him I am comforting my inconsolable wife and will try to call him back. She lets me know he is not happy. She looks pleased.

In three hours, the call comes in. Our girls have been dropped off in a park near the Chesapeake Bay Bridge.

Neither we or Hal and Jordan are permitted to ride to the park with the FBI agents, but we can be nearby to see the girls as soon as the FBI brings them from the park.

We have won. I sense publicity about the AG's admission to me can be the beginning of the end of the so-called project to 'protect' children by separating them from their parents. I plan to make amends for my role in it for the rest of my life.

CHAPTER TWENTY-NINE
THE REPORTER

Wednesday Evening, Washington DC

I spent two days doing interviews as a source rather than interviewer, and I prefer the latter. My editor went to the publisher with my proposed suspension – for showing bias while preparing a story -- and it was torn up. He gave me the pieces.

People continue to congratulate me on the release of Joe Delaney's daughter and her friend, as they did when Bill and Annie picked up Corozón and Pico at the Children's Holding Center. I don't feel like a winner. If anyone is, it's Juan Gomez. His photo woke up any American eyes that tried not to see the child seizures.

I recommended that the *Post* hire Gomez. CNN and the *Dallas Morning News* and *LA Times* did lengthy interviews with him. He'd probably rather work out west.

But Isabella is still dead, and her kids will be scarred for life. They were assigned to Bill and Annie Haines' custody quickly because their mother died while in custody and Uncle Sam didn't want to answer 5,000 more questions about them. Minus their mother, but not in cages or behind barbed wire.

President Diamond's own children will continue to tweet photos of their beautiful children in beautiful clothes, being hugged by their trendy parents. I don't begrudge their happiness, only that they flaunt it in the wake of the tragedies their father creates.

As I drive toward my home in Takoma Park, Maryland, my editor calls. The president has signed an executive order stopping the seizures. He says he is ending a sixty-year old problem.

"Gee, if that were true, let's see. Twenty-three hundred kids every six weeks. I wonder where the prior administrations have hidden all of them?" In full sarcasm mode, I ask my editor his opinion on this.

He refers to a broad part of the president's anatomy. I laugh.

I have a serious question. "When will the 2,300 kids be reunited with their parents? Or aunts and uncles, whoever they came with or are looking for?"

He sighs. "Not only are no plans announced, it appears they have the option to keep doing this. I think they finally figured out they'd have nowhere to put all the kids if they do it to every family every day. They'll be more selective.

"So, kids stay in camps?"

"Wait a minute." He talks as he shuffles through papers. "They can be deported separate from their parents. Government only says they will 'try' to deport them together."

"What does Border Patrol say?"

More shuffling. "Gimme a minute. Here's what Border Patrol says, officially. 'For those children still in Border Patrol custody, we are reuniting them with parents or legal guardians returned to Border Patrol custody following prosecution.'"

I feel myself flush. "Prosecutions could take years."

"Yep. I think a lot of those kids are as screwed today as they were yesterday."

I make a U-turn. I have to start making calls. I won't quit until all the kids are back with their families.

EPILOGUE
CORZÓNE, PICO, THE COLONEL, AND ANNIE

Houston, Texas

Pico and I have lived in Texas for three months. We have many people who love us and take care of us, and I thank Colonel Bill and Annie every day. Uncle Bill and Aunt Annie. That's what we call them now.

I still miss Mamá and Papi so much. I understand why the bad men killed Papi, but I don't understand why the American bad men took Mamá. Uncle Bill says almost every person in America who wears a uniform is good.

I try to believe this, and when I say I can't, he shows me a picture of him and my Grandfather Tito when Uncle Bill wore his uniform. I believe Uncle Bill is good.

Pico is mostly happy. He only cries when Annie walks out of a room. He is usually okay when I go to my bedroom or the kitchen. It used to bother me that he didn't cry when I went away, but I decided when he drools on Annie he isn't drooling on me. She laughs when I tell her this.

Because I am so serious, Uncle Bill buys me a movie about a white lady who flies with an umbrella. He sings along with it when they laugh loud, and long, and clear.

I am learning English and I am learning to laugh. I start with smiling.

WHO ARE WE, REALLY?

Sometimes circumstances separate families. After their father's death in the early 1920s, my father and five of his siblings did a lot of their growing up in an Odd Fellows Home in Liberty, Missouri. At least they were together and saw their mother a few times a year.

Other times, political traumas (war, drugs, gang attacks, government persecution) tear families apart. Some people with stable lives help. Others look away.

In the worst of circumstances, the government itself orders children to be torn from their parents' arms. In Europe in the early to-mid 1940s, stronger kids could stay in the Nazi camps to work, younger ones were killed immediately. In our own country at that time, we put citizens in internment camps because their ancestors were from Japan, often many generations back. We let some young men out if they served in the U.S. military.

Family separation is not a 'recent century thing' in America. African American families brought to the U.S. against their will were regularly divided. It depended on whether the white slave owners could make more money by selling them separately. Many Native American children were taken from their parents and sent to boarding schools to make them "more like white people."

Most of us didn't expect such things to happen again.

Some of our families got to the land of the free before quotas, others try to come today to escape atrocities or seek a life for a family that has no food. The U.S. cannot accommodate everyone who wants to settle here. But we can set up fair processes that treat people kindly and do more than provide high-skilled employees largely to for-profit businesses.

If we don't want to treat everyone with dignity, we can change the Statue of Liberty from "give me your tired, your poor," to "welcome to the new America, land of me first and the hell with you and yours."

Elaine L. Orr

ABOUT THE AUTHOR

Elaine L. Orr usually writes light-hearted mysteries along with the occasional play or piece of reflective fiction. She used to travel overseas for work, sometimes to less-developed countries. She always returned with gratitude for the freedoms we have in the United States, and pride in its leaders. She has not recently traveled beyond U.S. borders.

www.elaineorr.com
www.elaineorr.blogspot.com

Made in the USA
Lexington, KY
27 November 2018